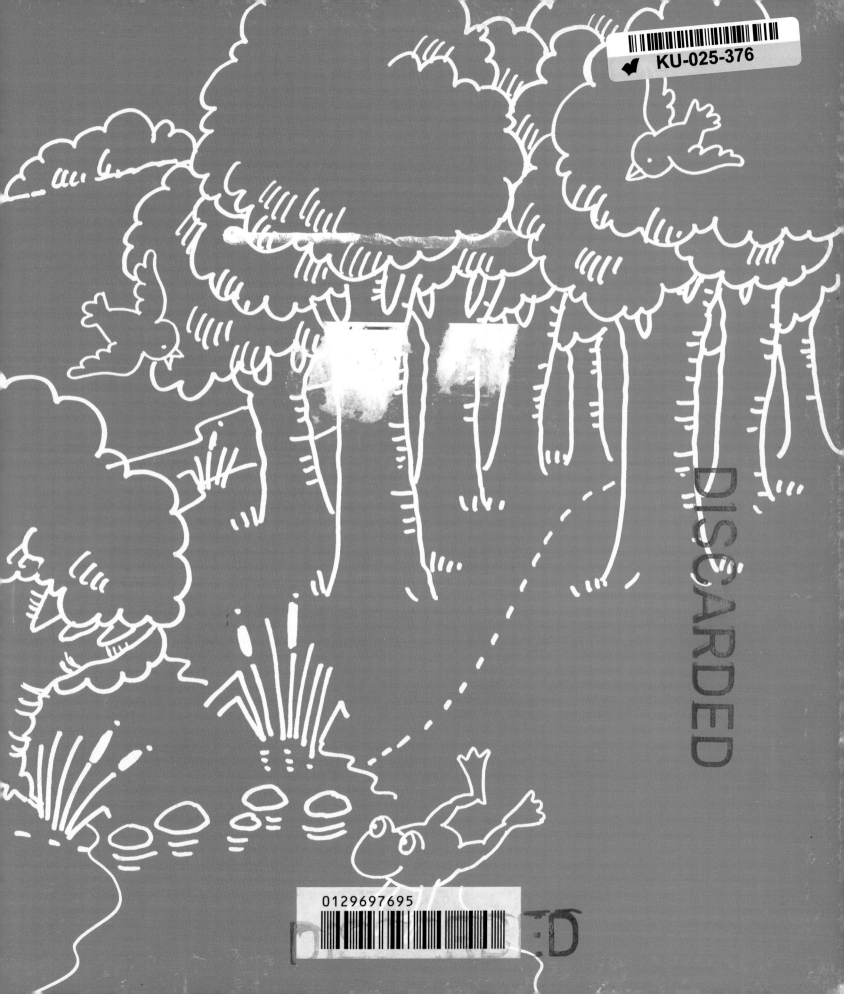

KU-025-376

DISCARDED

0129697695

DISCARDED

For my youngest granddaughter, Molly

T.M.

ORCHARD BOOKS

338 Euston Road, London NW1 3BH

Orchard Books Australia

Hachette Children's Books

Level 17/207 Kent Street, Sydney, NSW 2000, Australia

First published in Great Britain in 2006

Text and illustrations © Tony Maddox 2006

The right of Tony Maddox to be identified
as the author and illustrator of this work
has been asserted by him in accordance with
the Copyright, Designs and Patents Act, 1988.

A CIP catalogue record for this book is
available from the British Library.

ISBN 1 84362 015 4

1 3 5 7 9 10 8 6 4 2

Printed in China

www.orchardbooks.co.uk

Look Behind You, Oliver!

WARWICKSHIRE LIBRARY
& INFORMATION SERVICE

012969769 5

£10.99	16-Feb-07

Tony Maddox

ORCHARD BOOKS

It was a warm sunny day
on Mulberry Farm.

"It's a good day to go exploring!" said Oliver Owl.

"Can I come?" oinked Piggy Pig.

"Can I come, too?" quacked Dilly Duck.

"Can I come, too?"

"And me?" cheeped Little Chick.

"No," said Oliver. "You're too small to leave the farm. I'm going exploring all by myself!"

Oliver packed everything he might need for
an exploring kind of adventure, and set off.

"Let's follow him!" whispered
Piggy, Dilly and Little Chick.
"But don't let him see us!"

As Oliver swished through
the meadow, the bumblebees buzzed . . .

"Look behind you, Oliver!"

As he hopped across the stream,
the frogs croaked . . .

As he marched into the wood,
the birds chirped . . .

"Look behind you, Oliver!"

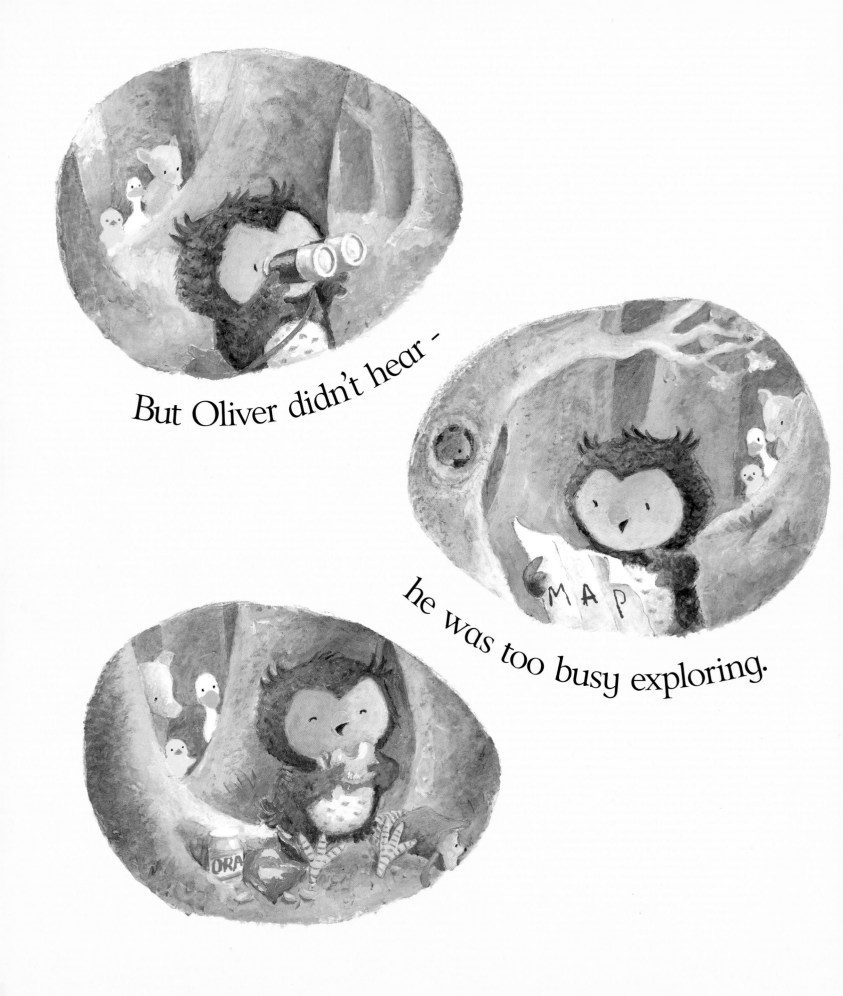

But Oliver didn't hear –

he was too busy exploring.

The deeper Oliver went into the wood,
the gloomier it became.
The trees grew taller
and the shadows
grew darker.

"I think I'll explore
my way back to the
farm," thought Oliver.

But then he realised that
he didn't know which way to go.
"I'm lost!" he cried. "How will I ever get home?"

All of a sudden, there was a shout . . .

"Look behind

"We followed you, Oliver,"
his friends explained.
"We wanted to go exploring, too!"

"I'm so happy to see you!"
smiled Oliver. "After all . . . adventures
with friends are the very best kind!"

Together, Piggy,
Dilly and Little
Chick . . .

. . . showed Oliver how
to get back to the farm,
exploring all the way.

"Thank you, everyone!" said Oliver.
"Now, what shall we play next?"

"Hide-and-seek!"
they all laughed.